S.W.I.T.C.H.

SERUM WHICH INSTIGATES TOTAL CELLULAR HIJACK

Grasshopper Glitch

Ali Sparkes

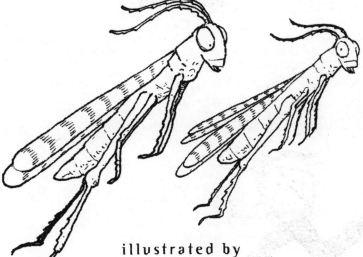

illustrated by
Ross Collins

OXFORD
UNIVERSITY PRESS

OXFORD
UNIVERSITY PRESS

Great Clarendon Street, Oxford OX2 6DP

Oxford University Press is a department of the University of Oxford.
It furthers the University's objective of excellence in research, scholarship,
and education by publishing worldwide in

Oxford   New York

Auckland   Cape Town   Dar es Salaam   Hong Kong   Karachi
Kuala Lumpur   Madrid   Melbourne   Mexico City   Nairobi
New Delhi   Shanghai   Taipei   Toronto

With offices in

Argentina   Austria   Brazil   Chile   Czech Republic   France   Greece
Guatemala   Hungary   Italy   Japan   Poland   Portugal   Singapore
South Korea   Switzerland   Thailand   Turkey   Ukraine   Vietnam

Oxford is a registered trade mark of Oxford University Press
in the UK and in certain other countries

British Library Cataloguing in Publication Data
Data available

ISBN: 978-0-19-272934-7
1 3 5 7 9 10 8 6 4 2

Printed in Great Britain

Paper used in the production of this book is a natural,
recyclable product made from wood grown in sustainable forests.
The manufacturing process conforms to the environmental
regulations of the country of origin.

For Elena

Danny and Josh
(and Piddle)

They might be twins but they're NOT the same! Josh loves insects, spiders, beetles and bugs. Danny can't stand them. Anything little with multiple legs freaks him out. So sharing a bedroom with Josh can be . . . erm . . . interesting. Mind you, they both love putting earwigs in big sister Jenny's pants drawer . . .

Danny

- FULL NAME: Danny Phillips
- AGE: 8 years
- HEIGHT: Taller than Josh
- FAVOURITE THING: Skateboarding
- WORST THING: Creepy-crawlies and tidying
- AMBITION: To be a stunt man

Josh

- FULL NAME: Josh Phillips
- AGE: 8 years
- HEIGHT: Taller than Danny
- FAVOURITE THING: Collecting insects
- WORST THING: Skateboarding
- AMBITION: To be an entomologist

Piddle

- FULL NAME: Piddle the dog Phillips
- AGE: 2 dog years
  (14 in human years)
- HEIGHT: Not very
- FAVOURITE THING: Chasing sticks
- WORST THING: Cats
- AMBITION: To bite a squirrel

CONTENTS

Twitchy Travellers

Danny was jumpy.

'Stop making that *noise*!' snapped Josh as they waited at the gate. Danny was making a peculiar screechy-scrapey noise through his teeth. He was trying to learn to whistle but he only managed to sound like a rusty bike chain being repeatedly dragged against a tin tray.

He didn't pay Josh any attention.

'Will you *stop* it!' Josh whacked his lunchbox against the back of Danny's head and his twin glared at him, rubbing his spiky blond hair.

'I can't help it. I'm nervous!' Danny muttered, eyeing the car at the roadside. The car which would take them to school this morning. Mum couldn't drive them in today and so their next-door neighbour, Petty Potts, was giving them a lift. She was just getting her bag from the house and soon they would be away.

Josh stared at the car too, and felt that his brother had some cause to be jumpy. Petty's car was so old it was actually made of *wood*. The back half of it looked like a chunk of old boat and the dark-green leather seats inside were like furniture from a museum. Piddle, their terrier dog, was cocking his leg against one of the back wheels.

'It can't be legal to drive this around on proper roads!' hissed Danny, as Petty emerged from her gate with a large open-topped woven straw bag in

her hands. 'I mean—do you think she's even got
a licence?'

'Come along, you two. Hop in,' said Petty,
opening the door and tipping up the front
passenger seat so they could get into the back.
'Oh, get away from my tyres, you nasty leaky
creature!' She glared at Piddle and he grinned up
at her doggily before shooting back into the garden
and up the side passage where they heard Mum
shutting the gate.

Petty tutted and went round to the driver's
door. She was in her brown raincoat and wearing
her usual tweedy hat, pulled down low over her
spectacles. She looked exactly like someone should
look, driving such an ancient wreck, thought
Danny. 'Pooh.' He pulled a face at Josh as they
clambered in across the bouncy cracked leather
seat. It also smelt like a museum.

'Where are the seatbelts?' asked Josh looking left
and right.

'It's a Morris Traveller, Josh,' said Petty, grinding
the gears as the engine coughed into life. 'They
didn't build them with seatbelts back in 1966. Just

hang on tight—I'm not going to crash.' She turned around, put her bag in between them on the seat, and creased her face into what she probably thought was a reassuring smile.

Petty Potts's reassuring smiles never really worked somehow. Danny grabbed on to a little leather strap above the window and narrowed his eyes at her.

Josh did the same.

'Oh, for heaven's sake, you two!' she huffed, as she turned back and started to drive up the road in a lurching fashion. 'You might have a little faith in me. I'm not going to kill you!'

Danny and Josh raised identical eyebrows at her in the rear-view mirror. Petty had never *tried* to kill them, true. But she had certainly brought them closer to a bizarre and grisly death than any other grown-up they knew. Since they'd stumbled into the secret underground laboratory hidden beneath her garden shed, they'd very nearly been crushed, drowned, splatted, pecked hollow, swatted, mummified and eaten—more times than they wanted to remember. Petty might *look* like a nice old biddy, but she was the genius inventor of SWITCH spray, which could change you into a creepy-crawly with just a few squirts. Josh and Danny had already been transformed into spiders and flies—and that was really quite enough.

Naming her *Serum Which Instigates Total Cellular Hijack* 'SWITCH' made it sound rather fun. And it was—if you didn't mind getting eaten, drowned, turned into soup or splattered with a giant sandal.

'Any more side effects from your house fly adventure?' Petty called back, cheerfully, over the rumble and clunk of the fifty-year-old engine.

'No. We've stopped sniffing around the bin now,' said Josh. 'And Danny hasn't spat on a doughnut or tried to walk up the kitchen window since last Tuesday.' He sighed and then grinned to himself. Being a bluebottle *was* very exciting. Even Danny had loved it—well, apart from the bit when he'd been on the lunch menu for a hungry spider.

'Good, good, good,' said Petty. 'You know, I thought it was a disaster when you two first accidentally ran into a jet of my Spider SWITCH spray . . . but actually it was the best thing that could have happened. If you hadn't found your way into my secret lab, I might never have moved on from trying to SWITCH rats and dogs!'

'Er . . . thanks,' muttered Josh, raising his eyebrows at Danny, who was shaking his head and looking annoyed. The dog Petty had been trying to spray was *their* dog, Piddle. It was when they were rescuing Piddle that they had first got caught in a jet of Petty's SWITCH spray.

'And, of course, rats could never tell me what the experience was like!' went on Petty. 'And you two are *so* helpful! I'm so delighted you've agreed to be my assistants on the S.W.I.T.C.H. project.'

'Look—we just said we'd help you out by looking for your missing cube things,' said Josh as they reached the traffic lights near their school. 'We're *not* trying out any more SWITCH sprays!'

'I never asked you to!' protested Petty, looking all innocent and injured. 'And finding my missing cubes is absolutely the most important thing. Without them I will never be able to rediscover my formula and move on to turning things into reptiles—and you'll never get the chance to find out how it feels to be a giant python or an anaconda or a Komodo dragon!'

'We don't *want* to find out!' squawked Danny. 'Haven't you heard us? Being turned into other creatures is just too dangerous!'

'Yes, of course, of course . . . ' Petty smiled ferociously into her rear-view mirror. 'Although I

can't imagine how anyone could hurt you if you were a twenty-four foot python!'

Danny and Josh looked at each other—and there was just the faintest twinkle of excitement in Josh's eyes. He thought about Petty's promise. If they could find the last four missing cubes which held the secret of the REPTOSWITCH spray, she would be able to temporarily turn them into amazing reptiles. Josh loved wildlife—being a lizard or a snake would be incredible! The BUGSWITCH was amazing enough but a REPTOSWITCH? It would be hard to resist trying *that* spray out. And nice to be less easy to eat or squash! This was a definite downside to being a creepy-crawly.

'Josh!' hissed Danny, narrowing his eyes at his brother. 'Don't even *think* about it! You don't even know she's telling the truth! She's as fishy as fishfingers in fish sauce in a fish-shaped dish!'

Josh had to admit Danny was right. Petty claimed some pretty mad things. Although she had the BUGSWITCH sprays sorted, she insisted a man who had worked with her had stolen the rest of her research and even burnt out bits of her memory. She'd forgotten where she'd hidden the special glass cubes which contained the secret REPTOSWITCH formula. That was why she needed their help—to find them. And they *had* found one.

'We have been looking for your cubes,' Danny was saying. 'And we will keep looking for them. But don't go thinking you'll *ever* change us into anything again—not unless we agree to it!'

'Well, of course not! What do you take me for? Some kind of monster?' huffed Petty. 'I would never dream of such a thing. But . . . I just wanted to tell you that I think I have perfected a SWITCH *potion* now. You can *drink* SWITCH instead of spray it on—and it'll have the same effect.'

'We're not drinking *anything*!' declared Josh.

'Of course you're not—but if you ever *did*, it's all quite safe because, look, there's a SWITCH antidote potion too! I made it just in case drinking SWITCH makes the changes last longer than the spray. It gets right inside, of course, so it probably lasts longer—but the antidote can stop it all at any time like the gas back in my lab. Look—I've got both the potion and the antidote in my bag.'

With one hand on the wheel, she turned around to rummage in the bag between them and was just hauling out a small plastic bottle when Josh shouted,

'LOOK OUT!'

There was a screech of elderly brakes and all three of them jerked violently forward as Petty's Morris Traveller nearly collided with the lollipop man. School bags, lunchboxes, and Petty's stuff went flying everywhere and it was just as well Josh and Danny had been hanging on to the little leather straps above their heads or they might well have shot through the windscreen.

Petty had bashed her nose on her steering wheel. 'Oh, all right! All right! Keep your stupid shiny hat on!' she was shouting at the lollipop man who was waving his yellow STOP sign around and looking very angry.

'Please—just drive around the corner, so we can get out,' wailed Josh keeping his head down behind the front seats in case anyone from their school was watching. He and Danny scrabbled about, picking up their bags and books and lunchboxes.

'My bun's all squashed!' moaned Danny, picking up a cake which now looked more like a biscuit.

'Well, mine had a pretty hard whack too, thanks for your concern!' sniffed Petty, as they pulled at last around the corner, away from the angry lollipop man.

'My buNNN! BuNNN—not BUM!' squawked Danny, with a horrified shudder.

'Thanks for the lift,' said Josh as they fumbled with the tipping front seat and the passenger door. He and Danny grabbed their school stuff and got out as fast as they could, slamming the door behind them.

Petty rubbed her nose, and called out, 'I'm off round the park to try the potion and the antidote out on the squirrels. I'll let you know how it goes!' and she did a violent U-turn, nearly knocking a passing postman off his bike.

'Come on,' said Danny, shoving his bottle of drink and flattened bun back into his lunchbox and slinging his bag over his shoulder. 'I never thought I'd say this, but I can't wait to get to school, where it's safe.'

And he went on through the school gates, having no idea that something very, very *un*safe was slurping about in his bag.

Bad Squash

'Who *is* making that noise?' snapped Miss Mellor.

Everyone in the class froze, widened their eyes and then looked around for the culprit. The room was silent.

'That scrapey, scratchy noise! It's really irritating,' went on Miss Mellor, putting down her spelling test marking, standing up and folding her arms.

'Don't know, Miss,' muttered a few innocent pupils.

Josh nudged Danny but his brother just shrugged.

'Well, whoever it was, stop it at once,' commanded Miss Mellor and sat down again, heavily, picking up her red pen while sending a warning glare around the classroom.

A few minutes passed as the class got on with 'quiet reading' and then the noise began again. Scratch-scrape. Scratch-scrape. Scratch-scrape.

Josh nudged Danny again, but his brother was engrossed in his book and quite unaware that he was moving his legs up and down against each other. The seams of his new school trousers and the Velcro tabs in his school shoes kept scraping and scratching.

'Miss—*Miss*! It's him! It's Danny,' called Claudia Petherwaite, pointing at her classmate with a smug look on her face. Josh narrowed his eyes at her.

'Danny—what on earth are you doing?' demanded Miss Mellor. 'You sound like some kind of insect!'

'Sorry, Miss,' mumbled Danny, looking a little pink. 'I didn't know I was doing it.'

'Well, now you *do*, stop it!' She sat down again and snatched up her pen once more. She was not in a good mood.

Claudia smirked at Danny who poked his tongue out at her. He managed to keep quiet for the rest of the lesson.

Just before lunch Miss Mellor stood up and did a sudden lunchbox check. All that week, the school had been working on a healthy eating project. Those who brought in sandwiches had to show what was in their lunchboxes and get a score out of ten for how healthy it was.

Those who had school dinners sat back and watched—*they* didn't have to go through this. But about fifteen others went to get their lunchboxes and open them up for inspection.

'Not bad, Billy,' said Miss Mellor, peering into Billy Sutter's plastic tub. 'Egg and cress. *White* bread though—should be wholemeal really . . . raisins . . . good . . .'

Josh and Danny peered anxiously into their lunchboxes. Their lunches were as identical as they were. Ham sandwiches, grapes, a bit of cake, and a small bottle of lemon squash. The bread was white though.

'Claudia, what's in yours?' asked Miss Mellor. Claudia opened her little basket-weave box as if it was a birthday present.

'I've got home-made wholemeal rolls, filled with organic roasted vegetables and low-fat hummus,' she declared proudly.

'Hummus? Isn't that something you get off the compost heap?' hissed Danny, as Miss Mellor clucked approvingly at Claudia.

'And I have crudités,' went on Claudia, holding aloft a little bundle of cut up carrot and cucumber sticks. 'With wild mushrooms and couscous.'

'Couscous? Sounds like the cat bringing up furballs,' muttered Danny.

'Looks like it too,' said Josh as Claudia held out something sludgy in a dainty plastic dish.

'And what do you have for dessert?' asked Miss Mellor.

'Oh, Mummy doesn't give me a dessert,' said Claudia, glowing with pride. 'She says sugar rots my teeth. I *do* nibble on sun-dried mango—but only at weekends.'

'Gosh.' Even Miss Mellor looked slightly appalled. 'And to drink . . . ?'

'Just water, of course. Squash is full of sugar . . . and the sugar-free stuff kills children's brain cells,' explained Claudia, closing her lunchbox with a satisfied snap.

Miss Mellor moved on to Danny and Josh with a rather fixed grin. Then she peered down into their open lunchboxes. 'Hmm . . . that looks OK. Some fruit. White bread, though—tsk! And cake?'

'There are raisins in it!' said Josh hopefully, but Miss Mellor's lips didn't unpurse. She lifted Danny's plastic bottle out. 'Squash?'

'Yep. Lemon,' said Danny, with a cheeky grin. 'Full of sugar! Yeah!'

'Your teeth will drop out!' cooed Claudia, happily, as the bell for lunch rang.

'I'll risk it!' said Danny, as Miss Mellor went back to her desk, and he unscrewed the bottle and took a slurp. 'Eeeeuurrgh!' he spluttered. 'This isn't

our usual squash! Yuck! Mum must have got some different stuff by mistake.'

Josh, having put his school work into his drawer, was now unwrapping his sandwiches. The 'packed lunchers' ate at their desks while the school dinners crowd went off to the hall. 'Better just get some water from the sink in the toilets, then,' he said.

Danny didn't say anything.

Josh took a big bite of sandwich. 'Great ham, though,' he mumbled, with his mouth full. 'Ham's my favourite. What's yours?'

'Chirrup.'

Josh looked around at the chair next to him. Danny's lunchbox was open and his sandwiches half unwrapped. His bottle of yucky squash still had its lid off. Danny was nowhere to be seen. He must have gone for water.

But sitting on his blue plastic seat, chirruping, was a bright green grasshopper. Josh grinned. That'd give him a scare when he got back.

It was only a matter of seconds before the screaming started. Daisy and Emily spotted the grasshopper first, when it suddenly launched itself through the air and landed on their table.

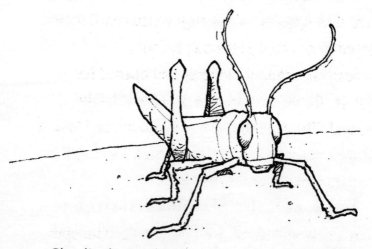

Claudia dropped her couscous and began to squeal, backing away from the long-legged beast crouching on the nearby desk.

'What *is* going on?' demanded Miss Mellor.

'Eeeeeeeuw! It's a grasshopper! A grasshopper!' shrieked Daisy, Emily, and Claudia. Several other girls began to scream now, as the grasshopper launched itself up into the air and landed, half a second later, on Miss Mellor's desk. Craig Thomas, who was standing nearby, also gave a little shriek, which he tried to turn into a cough. Three or four other boys were looking very uneasy.

'Josh!' called Miss Mellor, looking rather edgy herself. 'Can you catch it, please?' Everyone knew that Josh was mad about creepy-crawlies. Danny called him 'a freaky little bug boffin'.

Josh ran across to her desk and opened his hands. 'Come on . . . come on, little fella!' he coaxed. The grasshopper turned around and looked at him. It rubbed its impressive back legs together and chirruped again.

Josh wished that Danny was there to see it. It was a beautiful shiny green meadow grasshopper, with a rather endearing way of tilting its shiny green head and waving its shiny green front legs.

Almost as if it was trying to say something
to him!

'Danny, come and see this!' called out Josh
glancing around the room, but there was still no
sign of his brother. Danny might have freaked out
anyway—he didn't like grasshoppers.

The grasshopper waved harder. It was doing a
little dance now! Amazing! If Danny were here
he'd have stopped being scared by now, and would
be laughing! He'd be waving back! He'd be . . .

Josh suddenly felt cold. His eyes bulged. He was
replaying something in his mind. The near-crash in
Petty Potts's car that morning. All the lunchbox stuff
and the bits and pieces in Petty's bag, flying around.
Then he saw Petty talking to them . . . telling them
about the drinkable SWITCH potion, which she was
taking to the park.

Josh stared back at Danny's desk, at the open
bottle. He could see that it was not the same bottle
as his own—and their bottles, like the rest of their
lunch, were normally identical.

OH NO! yelled a loud, panicky voice in his head.
DANNY! DANNY DRANK SWITCH POTION!

'Well, go on then, Josh,' said Miss Mellor. 'Pick it up! I want it off my desk!' Four or five curious classmates had now clustered around Josh. The grasshopper was still waving at him. Rather frantically.

'Danny!' Josh whispered, holding out his palm. 'Get on my hand!'

'Just pick it *up*, Josh,' snapped his teacher. 'Before it hops off somewhere else.'

'No bovver, Miss,' said Billy Sutter, holding a heavy maths book. 'I'll get it.'

And before Josh could start to scream '*NOOOOO!*' he'd slammed the book down.

Toilet Trouble

'DANNEEEEE!' shrieked Josh, horrified. The classmates who had crowded around, ghoulishly waiting to see the mashed insect, wondered why Josh was shrieking for his brother.

With a trembling hand, Josh reached out and lifted the heavy book. He gulped hard and tears blurred his vision as he steeled himself to witness Danny squished flat all over Miss Mellor's ink-stained desk.

The book lifted and the rest of the class held its breath. Underneath was . . .

'Nuffin'! It must have hopped off!' grumbled Billy, disappointed.

'There it is! On Josh's hair!' squealed Daisy, and Billy picked up the book, ready to thwack it down on Josh's head. The grasshopper was too fast though. It shot across the room onto the bookshelf and then to the top of the paints cupboard. More screaming erupted. Then it landed on the windowsill and as Billy ran towards it, the heavy book raised up in one fist, it shot out through the open window.

'Phew! Drama over,' said Miss Mellor.

Josh stared out of the window, horror-struck, as Miss Mellor turned to write on the whiteboard. Then he ran back to Danny's desk, grabbed the bottle and screwed its lid on tight before running back across the classroom and jumping up onto the low windowsill. Outside, a paving stone path led past the window, and on the other side of it the school playing field stretched away towards some trees and bushes.

Danny could be anywhere! Josh looked behind him but the remaining kids in the class were getting on with their lunch now and Miss Mellor still had her back to him. Josh didn't wait any longer. He jumped out of the window, landing on the path, and then ran out onto the playing field.

'Danny!' he shouted, desperately staring around the grass and bushes. 'Danny! Where are you?'

He listened hard, but all he could hear were the shrieks of kids in the upper school playground.

Even if Danny was chirruping at the top of his voice, there was no way Josh would hear him. Josh sank to his knees and put his face right into the grass. 'DAANNNEEEEE!' he wailed into it, knowing it was hopeless. His brother could be anywhere—worse, he might already be inside a blackbird.

Then something pinged against his ear. He lifted his head and Danny dropped onto his open palm. At least, he thought it was Danny. It could be another grasshopper.

'Danny?' murmured Josh waving a finger at the insect. It waved its short feelers back. 'It is you . . . isn't it?!' The grasshopper waved again. 'OK—if that's you, waggle your left feeler!' The insect did and Josh heaved a huge sigh of relief, which nearly blew Danny back into the grass.

'What are we going to do? You drank SWITCH potion! And we've got maths in half an hour. How am I going to explain this to Miss Mellor?'

Danny offered up a number of suggestions. He scraped his back legs and wings together frantically, creating that chirruping noise, and it was clear that he had quite a lot to say. But Josh couldn't understand a word of it. He stared anxiously around the playing field and clutched the potion bottle in one hand, wondering what on earth to do. If only one of them had also picked up the antidote! He knew he hadn't—he'd drunk some of his squash and it was the usual stuff.

'Wait, though—Petty took antidote with her to the park,' he said. 'Maybe she's still there! It's not far away . . . Yes! That's the answer. We have to get to Petty. I reckon I can make it there in five minutes if I run . . .'

Josh stood up, Danny cupped in his hand, and made for the school gate which led off from the playing field and out into the lane. The park was only a short walk away. Petty might well be there still, wondering why the lemon squash wasn't working on the squirrels.

Desperately hoping no teacher or dinner lady would notice him, Josh ran along the edge of the

boys' toilet block towards the school gate. But as
he reached the corner of the low red-brick building,
Billy Sutter and his friend Jason Bilk stepped out
and bumped into him.

'OI! Watch where you're going!' grunted Jason.
Billy noticed immediately that Josh had something
in his hand.

'Wassat then?' he asked, prodding a muddy
finger at Josh's closed hand. A chirrup came from
inside it. 'You got that grasshopper again? You made
it a pet or summink?' Billy and Jason prised open
Josh's hand, despite his squawks of protest and
Danny looked up, waggling his feelers anxiously.

'I'm gonna get it this time!' chuckled Billy and slapped his hand down—but Danny had shot away like a green rubber band before he could be squashed. Now he was on the floor by the boys' toilets door. At once Jason and Billy started trying to stamp on him.

'NO! LEAVE HIM ALONE!' shrieked Josh and chased them into the toilet block where Danny had jumped next. Billy and Jason were clomping about wildly all over the damp concrete floor, shouting 'Squash it! Squash it!' Josh stood, aghast, feeling totally helpless. Then there was a flicker of movement and he spotted his brother in a cubicle. Josh threw himself inside it, slamming the door behind him. He firmly locked it as Danny leapt onto the toilet roll holder, looking very agitated.

'Are you OK?' hissed Josh—just as there was a break in the stamping and both boys outside heard him clearly. They let out peals of laughter.

'Oh—wittle Hoppy Woppy! Are you hurt?' said Jason, in a drippy voice. Billy squealed with mirth.

'Come on—come out! Bring out your little pet!' chortled Jason. 'We'll only stamp on him once.'

Josh hoped if he just said nothing they might get bored and go away, but five minutes later they were still banging on the toilet door and jeering. If they kept this up much longer there would be no time to get to the park and find Petty before he and Danny were meant to be back in class—and they'd be in big trouble. He could just wait here, hoping that Danny would switch back again, but he had no idea how long it might take. Petty hadn't known either—that's why she'd made the antidote. And if Danny did suddenly switch back, how would they explain it to the two boys outside the cubicle? The high narrow window was way too small for anyone to crawl in or out of.

'OI—GIVE US A LEG UP!' said Billy.

Josh groaned.

There had to be some way out of this. Then he blinked and stared at the bottle in his hand. There it was. The only escape. He put Danny up on the ledge by the window, which was slightly open. As two rows of fingers hooked over the top of the toilet door with a thud, he unscrewed the bottle's lid, and drank two gulps.

As the grunts and scuffles on the other side got
louder, he put the lid back on and hid the bottle
behind the toilet.

Seconds later, Billy, puffing with effort, peered
down into the cubicle with confusion.

Josh had vanished.

A Whisker from Death

'WHEEEEEEEEEEEEEEEEEEE!' yelled Josh as he
flung himself through the air. His back legs were
like a huge slingshot, shooting him high above
the forest of grass below him—only the slingshot
came along for the ride too.

'It's brilliant, isn't it?' called back Danny,
who'd had twelve minutes more practice at being
a grasshopper than his brother. 'As soon as I
switched I just had to jump! Even though I was
scared—I just had to! We can fly, too! See—we're
flying!' The stiff little wings on his back opened
out like a short green cape, helping him to glide
on and on through the warm air. They were already
out of the school. They'd jumped down from the
toilet window, across the field and over the high
boundary hedge without any problem at all.

'This is the best creepy-crawly we've been yet!' laughed Josh opening out his own wings and gliding along behind Danny. Far below him flashed a green garden and a blur of blue-white pond. Insects the size of dogs flew past them, some making noises like small jets, others more like helicopters.

THWUMP! THWUMP! They landed side by side on a grey brick wall and turned to inspect each other's shiny new grasshopper bodies. They each had two sets of fairly normal-sized insect legs which were surprisingly muscular with little hooky feet—or hands. But their hind legs were three times bigger and bent back behind them in a upside-down V. Their eyes were large and round, with short feelers set above them like pointy eyebrows. Josh thought Danny's long face looked rather solemn, until his brother started wiggling his little finger-like mouth parts about with enthusiasm.

'What are Billy and Jason going to think when they find you've disappeared?' he giggled, in a voice not too unlike his own considering he had a grasshopper's mouth.

'I'm more worried about what Miss Mellor will think. We could get detention for a week!' said Josh, rubbing his legs nervously against his wings.

'Ooh!' Making the noise himself, it was incredibly loud and croaky. 'That's how grasshoppers make their chirruping noise!'

'Careful,' said Danny, looking around. 'It's bad enough being chased by stupid kids who want to squash you. You don't want to attract predators too! What eats grasshoppers, Josh?'

Josh gulped. 'Well . . . we don't taste great. That's why we're quite bright green and shiny. It's to warn anything that wants to eat us that we're a bit—I dunno—sour. We're still not safe though. Birds, mice, snakes, spiders—all the usual ones— they'll have a go if they can. We should keep moving. We need to get the antidote.'

Danny nodded. 'Which way, do you think?'

'That way,' said Josh waving his feelers firmly to his left. He didn't know how he could be so sure . . . it was something to do with the way the sun was shining and the smell in the air. He felt a rumble inside him. He hadn't had much lunch.

'I'm starving,' said Danny, as they catapulted themselves high into the air again. Of course, *he* hadn't had any lunch at all. 'Wooooo-hooo! Oh yeah! No, I'm really hungry . . .'

'Of course,' called Josh now flying alongside his brother with his rather dashing green cloak wings. 'Grasshoppers are big eaters. They eat at least sixteen times their own body weight—every day! I'm hungry too. But we can't stop.'

Three seconds later they stopped. They landed
on a large leafy bush which grew up against a low
brick wall. It smelt as good to them as a doughnut
factory at tea time. Josh found himself cramming
his mouth with thick juicy chunks of green leaf.

Danny settled on a leaf next to him and also
began to demolish it with loud chomping noises.

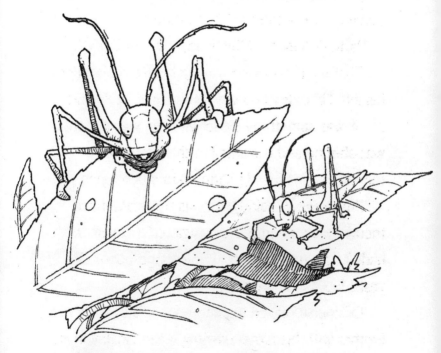

'Ooooooh, this is so good!' munched Danny.
'How come we never ate leaves before? There's
loads in our garden! We just ignore them . . . '

When the empty feeling inside him began
to ease off, Josh looked up. He was surprised to
see that Danny had stopped eating. Danny's big
green eyes were bulging. Suddenly Danny spat
out something brown and sticky right onto his
lovely leaf.

'EUURGH! MANNERS, PLEASE!' said Josh. 'Did
you eat a nasty bit?'

Danny shook his head and stared at Josh, his
enormous eyes shining like glass beads. Somewhere
in his brain Josh knew that spitting brown stuff
was a bad sign. It was something grasshoppers did
when—

'JUMP!' yelled Danny before he pinged up into
the sky. Which helped Josh to remember. Ah
yes . . . grasshoppers chucked up brown goo out
of fear. Usually fear of . . . PREDATORS!

All Josh saw, when he finally turned around,
was a huge mouth—a gigantic pink diamond
shaped pair of jaws with sharp white fangs and a
pointed pink tongue with hundreds of spikes on it.
Blecch! He spat out his own brown blob.

His slingshot legs threw him high into the air,

but then he collided, with a whump, against a thick furry log, which was falling from the sky.

When five razor-sharp white claws shot out of it, Josh realized that it was actually a paw.

He found himself splatted back down on the leafy wall, with a gigantic furry face pressed right against him. A moist pink nose nudged him and a fan of fine white spiky things drooped down on either side of him. Whiskers. A gust of meaty breath blew him over.

Josh realized he was about to be eaten by a cat.

In Ear

High above Josh, Danny clung to a springy twig
and stared down in horror at the enormous furry
monster that was sniffing and biffing at his brother.

'JOOOOOOOOOOOSH!' he bellowed, but
he couldn't hear anything except a scarily loud
thrumming, wheezing noise. He realized it was the
cat. The cat was purring! Poor Josh. He liked cats.
So did Danny. Usually cats purred when they were
getting some milk or being stroked—not when
they were about to bite you in half.

Danny jumped down onto the cat's head. He
landed up to his armpits (or legpits, depending on
how you looked at it) in thick tabby fur. The cat's
right ear flicked once, but it was so fascinated by its
prey it didn't try to shake Danny off. Hanging on to
the fur, Danny leaned out to see if Josh was OK.

At least he couldn't feel, hear or—worse—smell the cat chewing on anything.

Far below he could see Josh trying to crawl away from the cat's paw, so he could jump away, but the cat kept following him along the top of the wall, keeping its paws or nose just above him, so he couldn't escape.

'JOSH!' yelled Danny, tilting his head back so he could hear better (his ears, it turned out, were on his belly). 'Are you all right?'

'Yes—but I can't jump away. It's playing cat and mouse with me!' shouted back Josh.

'Maybe it won't eat you,' called Danny, trying not to squeak with fright. 'Maybe it just wants to play.'

'Oh yes—that'll be it,' squawked Josh dodging a claw as it swiped past his feelers. 'It only wants to be friends! In a "slash my head off" kind of way. That's nice then.'

Danny racked his brain, trying to work out what he could do. How could he distract the cat? He edged over its brow and wondered about jumping into its eye, but a thicket of eyebrow hairs, almost as long as its whiskers, sprouted out above the nearest glinting green orb. He'd never get past that before he got a claw stuck through his innards.

What about the ear though?

He hopped across to a triangular tent of cat skin and peered around the edge of it. It was a bit like a teepee inside, with tufts of fine fur lightly covering soft pink and grey skin. It was quite cosy, really, even though it was waggling about a bit as the cat's head switched from side to side, eagerly watching the tormented victim between its paws. There was even a pet in the ear tent—a surprised looking flea which was drinking what looked like Ribena through a straw poked somewhere down inside the tufty fur. The flea stared at Danny and paused, mid-slurp. There was a small pop and the straw snapped back into its brown shiny face. It burped. 'Pardon!' it said, waving a short hairy black foreleg in front of its mouth parts.

'Better out than in,' said Danny.

'EEEAAARGH!' shrieked Josh below. The cat's mouth was descending on him again, its spiky pale pink tongue scooping out to flip him back between its razor sharp teeth. He could see the roof of its mouth, a dome of tough wet ribbed skin, and knew he would be mashed against it any second now.

Danny lost no time. He jumped into the cat's ear and started rubbing his legs and wings together in a frenzy. The noise, in the confined space, was deafening. The flea hopped out in an instant.

'MEEEEEEEEEEEEEAAAAAAAAAH!' yowled the cat and flipped over like a furry tiddlywink, pounding both paws against its ear. Danny shot clear with just a millisecond to spare. Josh flipped up past him, looking very . . . well . . . green.

'Th-that . . . was t-too . . . c-close,' he stuttered as they flew away. 'I was just about to be cat chewing gum.'

They both shuddered with relief as they flew
down over the fence around the park.

'We've got to get to Petty. We can't risk any
more stops,' said Josh looking left and right as they
glided low across the grass. 'It's not safe down
there!'

VROOOOOM! Danny ducked in the air and swooped sideways as a dark shadow flitted past him. 'It's not safe up here, either!' he yelled. He looked up to see a dark flash of feathers and claws zooming around in a circle above them. A starling. Its sleek oil-coloured feathers glinted in the sun as it turned back to have another go at pecking him out of the air.

'DOWN!' shrieked Josh and dropped like a stone into the grass. Danny followed. Two thuds later they were hidden in a thicket of green which rose just above their heads. Breathlessly they crouched

and waited. 'Don't move!' whispered Josh. 'It will only see us if we move.' The starling swooped low over the grass, made an ear-splitting screechy noise and then flew away.

'It didn't see us!' gasped Danny. 'It couldn't make us out. Look—we're exactly the same colour as the grass!'

'Camouflage,' said Josh. His feelers quivered with shock. 'We're meadow grasshoppers. Designed to look nearly invisible in grass.'

'OK, so we're quite safe here then,' sighed Danny. 'But how are we ever going to find Petty Potts if we can't leap up and look around? And what time is it? We'll be late back to school and then we'll be in trouble. Oh—this is so not good! I thought we might get to have a bit of fun for a change, but oh no, we're just fast-food with feelers, as usual. I'm freaked out, I am.'

He spat out another blob of brown goo. 'Sorry.'

Sit Tight

Petty Potts was annoyed. She'd managed to entice three or four squirrels over to her bench in the last hour and each of them had scampered off with her special peanuts.

She knew, obviously, that there wasn't much point in trying to get a squirrel to swig a bit of dodgy looking potion out of a plastic bottle. No, she had taken a tin cup along in her bag and put a little of the potion into it before dropping some peanuts in and making them good and SWITCHy. Then she set the peanuts down, one by one, at the far end of the wooden park bench, and waited for the cheeky squirrels to show up and nick them. She had been careful to wear disposable plastic gloves. She had no intention of SWITCHing herself! One day she might, but she was quite old and might not recover from it.

Petty dug deep into her coat pocket and pulled out a little green velvet box. Opening it up, she gazed wistfully at the two shining glass cubes inside it. She picked up one of them and held it up to the light. It sparkled in the sun, and the hologram of a tiny lizard could be clearly seen inside it.

'One out of six!' she sighed. She put the cube
back in the box, next to the other cube, which
had a slightly different hologram inside it, with a
sigh. 'Two out of six. Which adds up to one third
of the formula to make REPTOSWITCH. Well, I'm
glad to have you two,' she murmured at the cubes,
'but what about the other four, eh? Where did I
hide the others? If only that scurrilous waste of
space Victor Crouch hadn't burnt out my memory,
I would know! I'd have the bug formula and the
reptile formula. There might even be mammal or
bird formula one day, for all I know! But if Josh and
Danny don't find the rest of your little cube family,
I may never know!'

Nobody was nearby to hear Petty talking to
herself, which was probably just as well. Petty
talked to herself quite a lot. She found it was the
only way to get an intelligent answer.

'Of course, they don't understand how
important this is. I am changing the world! But
all they're worried about is getting to school on
time. Honestly! Children today have no sense of
adventure.'

Petty snapped the little green box shut, put it on her lap, and trained her binoculars back onto the little family of four squirrels which were running around a warm patch of grass beneath the oak trees. Still no change. Obviously the potion wasn't working as well as the spray. Those squirrels should be hopping about looking very green and confused by now—getting panicky about their sudden lack of bushy tails.

If only she could see just one grasshopper! 'AAAAAAAAAARRRGGGHHHH!' Suddenly a huge grasshopper loomed in front of her. It took a second or two of frantic flapping around her head before Petty realized she was still looking through the binoculars—and the grasshopper was right on the lens.

'You mad old baggage!' she scolded herself and then turned the binoculars around to peer at the insect on the lens. Maybe the potion had worked after all! But . . . no . . . all four squirrels were still racing around the grass.

'Just a proper grasshopper,' she muttered, flicking it away. It landed with a small click, by

her left shoe—and then started to disco dance. Another grasshopper hopped along and joined it, shimmying left and then right and then whirling its feelers in the air as if it was auditioning for *High School Musical.*

Unfortunately Petty wasn't looking. She was examining the SWITCH potion bottle more closely. Suddenly she slapped her palm against her forehead. 'You lunatic!' she said, crossly, to herself. 'You pudding-brained clod! This is the antidote! Not the potion. Now . . . ' she began to rummage in her bag, 'where did I put the potion? And why did I use two of the same kind of bottle? Tsk! Oh how annoying—the potion bottle must have dropped out in the car.'

'It's not working,' said Josh giving the disco dance routine a rest. 'She's not looking. We'll have to jump up on her knee. If we don't get that antidote soon we might never get back to school—or home—again!'

'Won't we just change back again anyway, after it's worn off?' said Danny. 'We did last time.'

'I don't know,' said Josh. 'This is the potion version, remember, not the spray. We've not ever drunk it before. It might last for ever for all we know! But if we stay out here much longer we'll just get eaten anyway. Oh will you stop that?'

'Sorry,' said Danny, kicking away another brown blob of panic goo.

'Come on—onto her knee!' said Josh and was just about to jump when a shadow fell across them. He looked up and saw the vast bulk of another human. 'Oh no! Someone's come and sat on the bench with her! We can't change back in front of someone else . . . even if we do get to the antidote!'

'Morning, Miss Potts,' shouted Mr Grant, who lived around the corner.

Petty sighed. 'Hello, Mr Grant.' The last thing she needed was some nosy neighbour interfering in her experiment. She put the bottle back into her bag.

'We have to get Petty to notice us!' insisted Danny. He glanced around nervously and gulped. 'I don't care who sees! I'm not staying here to get eaten.'

'Nice place to sit and watch the world go by, isn't it?' yelled Mr Grant. He was a bit deaf and didn't seem to realize that not everybody else was too.

'Hmm,' said Petty, trying not to wrinkle her nose. Mr Grant smelt of old tobacco and unwashed socks—and had fancied her for years.

'What's this then?'' shouted Mr Grant, suddenly picking the little green box up from the bench where it had slid from Petty's lap. He flipped it open without even asking and peered at the two glass cubes. 'Oh! Very pretty!' he grinned, showing off his dark yellow teeth.

'Do you mind?' Petty wrestled the box off him, and jammed it deep down into her coat pocket.

'I've got one of those on my mantelpiece,' belted out Mr Grant.

'I very much doubt it,' said Petty, crisply.

'Found it in a bird's nest!' he bawled on. 'A year ago, when I was cutting down my old hedge. Some magpie had got it. Gave it a wash and put it next to my clock, I did.'

Petty stared at him, her mouth open.

'Nice to find someone to share a bench with,' Mr Grant shouted, romantically. 'Especially at this time of day, when there's no screaming kids about. They should keep 'em all in school a bit longer, I say. Getting out at three? Nonsense. Lock 'em up with their teachers until six o'clock and give us oldies a chance to have a park bench to ourselves, eh? Ha ha ha!'

Petty was still trying to work out whether she had really heard Mr Grant say he had a SWITCH cube on his mantelpiece when two grasshoppers jumped up onto her knee and began to wave. Petty blinked and then her eyes stretched wide but she didn't say anything.

'Don't you think?' barked Mr Grant.

'Oh good lord,' said Petty, staring at her knee and suddenly realizing where the missing SWITCH potion must have ended up. 'It's Josh and Danny!'

'Don't you?' screamed Mr Grant. 'Don't you think it's nice here? No annoying kids—just you and me! Ha ha ha!' And he slapped his hand down on her knee.

Petty shrieked.

'Oh come on!' roared Mr Grant. 'I'm only being friendly!'

But Petty was staring in horror at her knee, where, only seconds before, Josh and Danny had been waving at her. That idiot Grant had surely just splatted them across her skirt.

She smacked his hand away and then gasped with relief. There was no sign of splatted insect. A chirruping noise made her look down at the little tin cup on the bit of bench between her and her nasty neighbour. Inside the cup there was still a puddle of antidote (which she had mistaken for potion) left over from the peanut dunking—and two grasshoppers were wallowing about in it.

'No need to be hoity-toity!' Mr Grant was shouting. 'I was only saying how nice it was to be here all on our own without any irritating, snotty-nosed schoolkids taking up all the benches and— DOOF!' Mr Grant was abruptly shoved sideways as two schoolkids appeared out of thin air on the bench between him and Petty Potts.

Petty hooted with laughter. Mr Grant fainted. By the time he'd regained his senses, he was alone. He took himself off to see the head doctor.

'Sorry the boys are late,' smiled Petty, putting her head around the classroom door as Josh and Danny sidled back to their desks. 'I had a bit of an emergency and they were helping me.'

'Oh,' said Miss Mellor, checking her watch. 'Well, it's only ten minutes. I suppose I don't have to mark it down. What kind of emergency?'

'They had to save me from something creepy-crawly! You know how good Josh is with that kind of thing,' said Petty, doing her best 'nice old dear' face as she pushed the SWITCH potion bottle deep into her straw bag. Josh had run into the toilet block to get it for her just before they came back into class.

'See you at home time, boys,' said Petty and hurried out of the classroom.

'You didn't eat lunch, either of you!' scolded Miss Mellor. 'Your lunchboxes are still out on your desks!'

'It's OK, Miss Mellor,' Danny grinned. 'We had a load of salad stuff while we were out. Couldn't eat another thing!'

'Really? Sounds very healthy,' said Miss Mellor, looking suspicious.

'It was!' said Josh. 'And we're going to eat more leaves when we get home. Even more than Claudia! We're going to scoff a whole hedge. It tastes great!'

Bug-Eyed Burglary

'You must be joking!' Danny held up his hands and shook his head. 'No way!'

'But you promised you'd help me!' insisted Petty. 'You said you would help me get back all my REPTOSWITCH cubes! Remember—you said you wanted to try out being a python one day—or a lizard—or an alligator!'

'We didn't say that! You did!' argued Josh.

'Oh nonsense!' Petty slammed the green velvet box down on her kitchen table. She had lured Josh and Danny in, as they arrived home from school, with the pretence that she was worried about them after yesterday's grasshopper adventure. 'I know you want to be an alligator, Josh! You're an eight-year-old boy, for heaven's sake. There would be something seriously wrong with you if you didn't!'

Josh looked at Danny. Petty was right. He did want to try out the REPTOSWITCH one day. Who wouldn't? Danny bit his lip. Josh knew his twin wanted to try it too.

Petty flicked open the box and pointed to the four empty dents where the missing SWITCH cubes belonged and fixed them with a fanatical stare. 'One more of these will mean we are halfway there! Halfway towards being able to switch humans into reptiles! Imagine what we could do with that! It's fantastic enough being able to switch you into insects and spiders—but imagine what you could do in reptile form!'

'OK—we said we'd help you look,' said Josh.

'And we have been helping. We've been all round your garden and our garden—and we always check out anything we see in the street that shines a bit like glass. But this is different. You're asking us to be burglars!'

'Oh, pee, pickle, and poo!' snorted Petty. 'I'm just asking you to take one teensy weensy sip of potion, to pop back to being a grasshopper, to jump through Mr Grant's letterbox and then to collect my SWITCH cube from his mantelpiece and come out with it. No harm done. He won't even notice.'

Josh and Danny looked at each other. There was only the slightest hint on their faces that maybe they might possibly think about Petty's plan—but she spotted it and immediately held up a tiny glass dropper, already filled with SWITCH potion. 'I've measured it out exactly for your height and weight and body mass,' she said, with an excited grin. 'It will last precisely ten minutes. Long enough for me to get you to the house and then to give you five minutes inside to find the cube, change back to your human form and get the cube back to me. Mr

Grant's out. Wednesday afternoon he always goes to the betting shop.'

Josh and Danny looked at each other again. Danny shrugged. 'Sounds simple enough.'

'EXCELLENT!' said Petty, holding up the dropper. 'TONGUES OUT!'

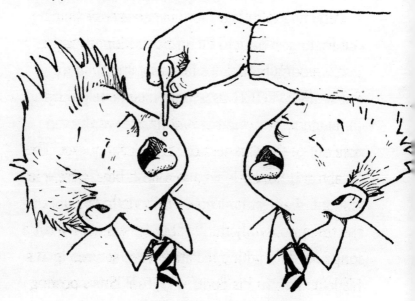

Petty hid them in her coat pocket, safely tucked into a small plastic tub with holes in the lid so there was plenty of air to breathe. It was not a pleasant journey, jogging along in the tub, which smelt of old curry.

'I hope she's right about this SWITCH cube

being in Mr Grant's house,' muttered Danny. 'We could be at home now, playing with Piddle or filling up the paddling pool—not stuck in a plastic tub in a mad old scientist's pocket, trying not to be sick. I'm only just holding back the panic goo here, you know!' His green face went a little greener.

Petty had told their mum her sons were helping out in the garden for half an hour. Mum thought that was a nice thing for Josh and Danny to do. She believed Petty was a lovely, harmless old lady.

Suddenly there was a flash of light as the tub rose out of the darkness of Petty's coat pocket. The lid abruptly snapped off and a fresh breeze blew in. Josh and Danny clambered warily up to the rim of the tub and saw that it was being held up against a long blue cliff, with a rectangle cave set into it. 'It's his letter box, in his door,' said Josh. 'She's posting us through!'

Sure enough, the dull yellow metal at the back of the 'cave' suddenly flapped backwards as Petty's enormous pink fingers poked at it. Josh and Danny leapt through the gap and found themselves gliding down through the cool indoor air of the hallway. They landed on the rough bristles of a doormat, next to a gigantic folded newspaper.

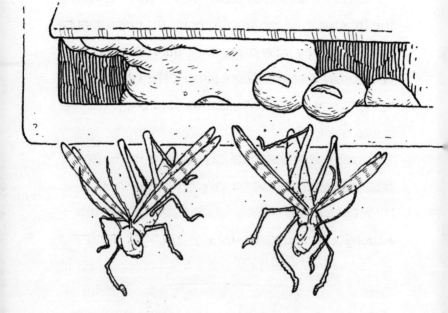

'BURGLARY ON THE INCREASE' read the front page headline, which made Josh and Danny feel guilty.

'Come on—we haven't got much time,' said Josh and sprang down the hallway and into the sitting room. He bounded up onto the mantelpiece above the fireplace in one easy leap. The long pine shelf was full of clutter: pictures, ornaments, matchboxes, tobacco tins, a pair of pliers, a jar of screws and lots of thick fluffy dust.

'Eeeuuw!' whimpered Danny. He was frozen on the other side of the jar of screws, his green mouth parts twitching with disgust. At his feet lay a large, upside-down spider. Hairy, crispy; the colour of straw, it was bigger than Danny. It was a good job it was dead.

'Just turn around and hop away!' advised Josh. He couldn't believe, after all Danny had been through, that he was still scared of a dead spider— although, he supposed, Danny *had* been the one

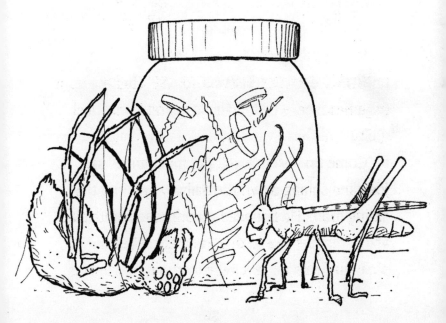

who was very nearly eaten by a spider a little while back.

Danny turned around and hopped away. Then he let out a chirrup of excitement. 'It's here! I've found it!'

Josh jumped along the mantelpiece and found his brother staring at a large, clear, perfectly cut cube of glass. Even through a layer of dust, it sparkled with rainbow light and inside, delicately carved by laser, was the hologram of a snake, its diamond-patterned body coiled like rope and its head raised up, as if ready to strike. 'It's beautiful,' murmured Danny. He wondered which bit was the one sixth of Petty's secret formula.

'It is,' agreed Josh. 'Uh-oh!' He felt a strange tingling and knew what was coming. 'Better get off the mantel—OW!' He sat up on the carpet, rubbing his head where it had smacked against the stone grate. 'That was a quick change!' He hadn't even had a second to hop down off the mantelpiece before he'd thwacked back into being a boy.

A moment later, Danny fell on his face.

'MMM-OW!' Josh shoved Danny off. 'You could've aimed somewhere else!'

'Sorry,' said Danny, as he picked himself up. 'Didn't have time.'

He turned and quickly collected the SWITCH cube from the mantelpiece, shoving it deep into his school trousers pocket.

'WHAT ON EARTH IS ALL THIS?' yelled a voice from the hallway.

Josh and Danny froze, horrified. They were in the middle of burgling Mr Grant's house—and he was IN IT!

Cubes, Cackling, and Cake

Mr Grant appeared in the doorway, looking furious—at the newspaper in his hand. He was staring at the headline and shaking his head.

'What's all this?' he thundered. 'Burglaries on the increase? Stuff and nonsense.' He flipped over the paper as two small burglars slid down behind his old leather armchair. 'Cricket club faces closure!' he bellowed. 'Rubbish! All newspapers are rubbish!'

Then he stomped across the room and thumped down into the armchair, sending up a cloud of dust around it. Josh and Danny, squashed behind it, held their breath and scrunched up their eyes. Josh felt a sneeze build up in his nose and pinched the end of it, desperately. If he sneezed they would be found out.

'Whoo-hoo!' called a voice and the doorbell clanged. Mr Grant, being rather deaf, had fitted an extra loud bell. 'Whoo-hoo!' called the voice again. It was Petty Potts, trying to sound sweet.

'What?' yelled Mr Grant, and hurried out to the door.

'She's distracting him so we can get out!' hissed Danny. He was right. As soon as the door was opened, Petty invited herself right in, and began to propel Mr Grant down the hallway, past the living room and on into the kitchen.

'I was wondering if you could lend me some TEA!' she was shouting. 'I've run out and I have friends coming. No time to run to the shops!' It was a pretty feeble excuse, but it was good enough for Josh and Danny. They sprang out from behind the armchair and dashed out through the hallway. Seconds later they were out on the pavement, hiding behind the front hedge.

'Thank you so much!' trilled Petty, as she backed away down Mr Grant's driveway. 'And really sorry about your funny turn in the park yesterday. I do hope it doesn't happen again. Real children are bad enough, without imaginary ones popping up on park benches!'

'Thanks!' mumbled Danny as all three of them ran down the road.

'Did you get it? Did you get it?' hissed Petty.

'Yes! Yes!' hissed back Danny.

'You might say thank you!' said Josh.

'Look, you're not the only ones who had to make a sacrifice!' huffed Petty. 'I had to agree to go to a beer and skittles night with Old Yellow Teeth, back there, to give you two enough time to escape!'

In Petty's kitchen, Danny took out the SWITCH cube and put it on the table.

'Oh, how wonderful!' sighed Petty, scooping it up and turning it over in her palm. 'Three out of six! We are halfway there!' She opened the green box and pressed the new cube in beside the other two. 'One day soon,' she murmured, standing straight and letting out a mad cackle, 'we will have them ALL! And then there will be NO STOPPING ME! Then I'll get you back, VICTOR CROUCH! I'LL GET YOU. I don't know how yet—but I'LL GET YOU!'

She was still shaking her fist, cackling and staring into the middle distance when she finally noticed Josh and Danny folding their arms and giving her a look.

'Any chance you can stop doing the evil genius thing now, and give us a bit of cake?' asked Danny.

'Oh, all right then,' said Petty.

DIARY ENTRY *592.4
SUBJECT: REPTOSWITCH CUBE RETRIEVAL

Excellent news! Working with Josh and Danny really paid off today, after I persuaded them to SWITCH into grasshoppers again and get into Yellow Teeth Grant's house to get back my third REPTOSWITCH cube.

Of course, it nearly all came a cropper when the smelly duffer turned out to be at home when he was meant to be out, but I managed to use the old Potts charm to distract him while the boys ran outside (note to self: have still got it!).

And also very useful to know that my calculations on how long the grasshopper spray would last were bang on!

REMEMBER

$$\frac{4 \times \pi^2}{0S-7*} \rightarrow \frac{\boxed{P_2}}{0.8} \times \frac{\sqrt{6}^2 \, 0/9}{9 \sqrt{5} \div} = \frac{4.178}{4.177} \, (548) \rightarrow$$

Amazed that I persuaded the boys to SWITCH again after their experiences yesterday. They nearly got stamped on and eaten by a cat this time. It would be rather unfortunate if they got squashed or digested before we get much further. I'm quite fond of them in a way, but imagine the blow to science!

Still, the idea of being a giant reptile one day seems to be keeping them keen. And speaking of giant reptiles, I am going to find out where Victor Crouch is working now. Maybe he is still in the secret government laboratories under Berkshire—and maybe I will be able to get back in. I bet he's still got that weird spiky black fingernail, but I wonder if he's grown any eyebrows back yet, after that body hair experiment went wrong . . . I hope not. A man like Victor Crouch doesn't deserve a decent set of eyebrows. One day, I am going to find him—confront him—and make him confess that he stole my work and burnt out my memory.

But in the meantime, as far as Josh and Danny are concerned, I will keep my promise and will never make them try any more spray or potion. Or trick them. Or bribe them. Or anything like that. Probably.

$$\frac{60}{OUP} \to \pi \to \cancel{\phi} \to \frac{1}{2}St^?$$

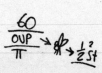

PLACES TO VISIT

Want to brush up on your bug knowledge?
Here's a list of places with special areas dedicated
to creepy-crawlies.

Liverpool Museum
http://www.liverpoolmuseums.org.uk/wml/
naturalworld/bughouse/

Marwell Wildlife Park
http://www.marwell.org.uk/

Natural History Museum
http://www.nhm.ac.uk/

Remember, you don't
need to go far to find
your favourite bugs.
Why not venture out
into your garden or the
park and see how many
different creatures
you can spot.

WEBSITES

Find out more about nature and wildlife using the websites below.

http://www.bbc.co.uk/cbbc/wild/

http://www.nhm.ac.uk/kids-only/

http://kids.nationalgeographic.com/

http://www.switch-books.co.uk/

Another exciting adventure awaits . . .

Entertaining Tarquin

'Guess what, boys?' Mum peered around the bedroom door with a grin.

Josh and Danny paused in their fight with rolled-up newspaper swords, and smiled innocently at her.

'What?' urged Danny.

The grin got stiffer. 'Tarquin's here to play!' Mum gulped. The looks on her twin sons' faces were so dark, it felt as if Hallowe'en had arrived early.

'*Tarquin*,' said Josh.

'*Here*,' said Danny.

Piddle the dog whined and shot under the bunk bed.

Danny threw down his sword, turned to Josh, opened out his arms and commanded: 'Through the heart. And make it quick.'

'Oh, come on! It'll be fun!' said Mum. 'Sshhh! He's coming up the stairs.'

They could clearly hear Tarquin approaching. He appeared to be singing opera.

'But we can't stand Tarquin!' hissed Danny, pushing his messy blond hair off his furrowed forehead. 'And you don't even like his mum! Remember how snotty she was about you winning the best garden contest?'

Mum sighed and said, in a low voice, 'I've let bygones be bygones! His mum needed help today. She's visiting a sick aunt. We have to look after each other—we're a community! Oh—here he is now!'

Tarquin trailed past her into Josh and Danny's room. At seven and a half he was nearly their age but he looked about fifty-five. He was dressed in neatly ironed trousers, a blue shirt, and a proper matching jacket. His hair was severely parted and combed flat to his head. His googly grey eyes narrowed as he examined their room. 'It's rather a mess, isn't it?' he said, in his peculiar high-pitched voice.

'Well, duh!' said Danny. 'It's a boys' room!'

'Yes,' said Tarquin. 'And so is mine. But I still refrain from growing fungus in it.' He eyed a jar of something gooey on the windowsill. The jar had once been filled with tadpoles, which Josh had set free in the garden pond last week. It had gone a little furry.

'Have fun, boys,' called Mum, already halfway downstairs.

Tarquin began to wander around, poking at their stuff. He prodded their comics and sniffed.

'So childish.'

Danny mouthed, '*Childish*? *Spiderman*?' at Josh and picked up his sword again. Josh frowned at him and shook his head.

'So what do *you* read then, Tarquin?' said Josh, trying hard to sound friendly.

'Oh—*Classical Music Magazine. New Scientist.* You wouldn't know them. I don't suppose you know anything about the arts or science.'

'We know a lot about science!' burst out Danny. 'We've had more science in the last six weeks than you've had in your life, you little—'

'Shut up, Danny,' said Josh. He was worried about what his brother might say next. Maybe he would tell Tarquin that he and Josh had been involved with scientific experiments so amazing that every scientist in the world would explode with astonishment if they knew. Maybe he'd boast that they'd been turned into spiders, then flies, and then grasshoppers over this year—after getting tangled up with the brilliant (but quite probably mad) old lady scientist next door.

Petty Potts seemed like a dotty old dear, but

she was in fact a genius. She had created SWITCH spray which could turn any creature into a creepy-crawly. She'd made a drinkable version too, and that was even stronger. What's more, if Josh and Danny managed to help her find the missing parts of her REPTOSWITCH formula, she could change them into alligators or giant pythons! It was a fantastic secret—and Josh was determined that Danny wouldn't blurt it out to Tarquin.

'Oh—don't be offended,' Tarquin was saying now, picking up Josh's magnifying glass from the top of their bookcase and turning it over in one hand. 'My mother says you can't help it that you're not as clever as me. It's not your fault.'

THWACK! Danny brought down his sword, aiming for the back of Tarquin's neatly combed head, but Josh caught it with an upswing of his own sword. 'Stop it!' he mouthed at Danny as Tarquin put down the magnifying glass and moved on.

'We do know quite a lot about science—especially nature,' said Josh. 'We know about creepy-crawlies. Let's take my magnifying glass outside and I'll show you some in the garden if you like.'

Tarquin shuddered. 'Eugh! If you show me a creepy-crawly I'll stamp on it.'

Josh was shocked. He was a great nature lover and had adored all kinds of creepy-crawlies long before he'd ever been one. Even Danny, who wasn't fond of them at all, would never deliberately squash one.

'You can't *tread* on them! That's just stupid!'

'No—sometimes I look at them first,' smirked Tarquin. 'It's quite fun to pull their legs off.'

'It's not fun for *them*!' said Josh, feeling quite hot in the face. He picked up his sword, ready to swing it into Tarquin's head, but this time Danny grabbed it, raised his eyebrows and waggled his finger at his brother.

Tarquin opened the door to their toy cupboard. Then he screamed.

FUN AND GAMES

There are more games for you to play and
download free on the S.W.I.T.C.H. website.
www.switch-books.co.uk

Word search

Search for the hidden words listed below:

SCHOOL	MR GRANT
SWITCH	FORMULA
CAT	HOLOGRAM
STARLING	JOSH
BILLY	DANNY

S	W	I	T	C	H	E	F	O	U
C	T	D	X	N	S	Q	O	P	V
H	A	A	C	L	O	G	R	H	D
O	C	N	R	S	J	A	M	P	O
O	G	N	P	L	F	D	U	T	I
L	K	Y	L	B	I	L	L	Y	K
D	A	B	A	N	G	N	A	U	I
C	L	A	R	E	V	L	G	E	Y
Q	J	H	O	L	O	G	R	A	M
M	R	G	R	A	N	T	L	U	R

Spot the difference

These pictures *look* the same, but can you spot ten differences?

Answers on page 118

True or false?

1) Grasshoppers have wings

2) Grasshoppers can eat 16 times their own body weight in a day

3) Some grasshoppers hear through their knees

4) Grasshoppers can leap 100 times the length of their own body

5) Grasshoppers spit out brown liquid when they are confronted with a predator

6) Grasshoppers eat other insects

7) Grasshoppers are an endangered species

8) Some grasshoppers don't have antennae

9) Grasshoppers eat flowers

10) Grasshoppers have four legs

Answers on page 118

Missing pieces

Can you work out which piece of the puzzle is missing?

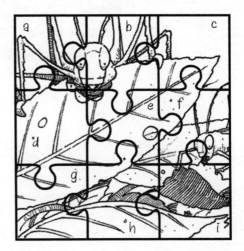

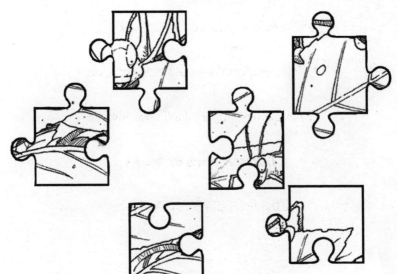

Answer on page 118

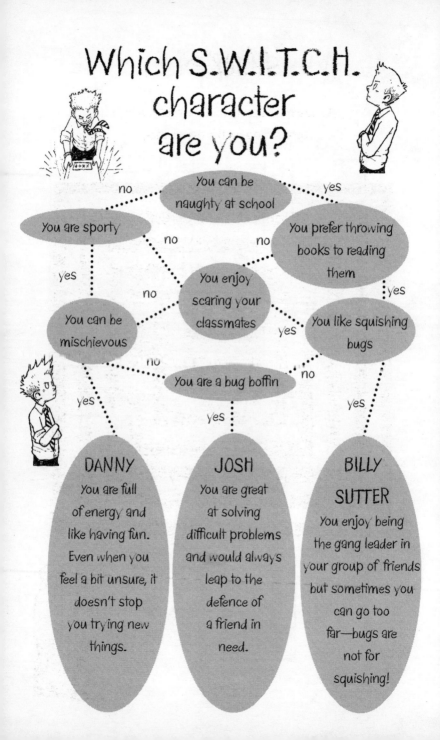

Maze

Help Josh and Danny find their way to Petty Potts, sitting on the park bench.

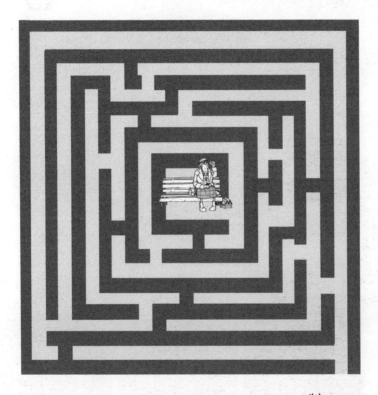

Answer on page 119

Board game

You have been turned into a grasshopper and must break into Mr Grant's house to find the missing REPTOSWITCH cube.

For this game you will need one die, a tiddlywink (or something of a similar size) for each player, and two or more players.

START The park 1	Bound ahead 2 squares. 2	 3
   6	 5	 4
Jump into the under-growth to hide from the cat. Go back 2 squares. 7	 8	You've been spotted by a starling. Go forward one square. 9
   12	You stop to munch on a leaf. Miss your next go. 11	 10
Hide from Petty's boots and miss your next go. 13	 14	**FINISH** Congratulations – you found the next REPTOSWITCH cube! 15

116

Are you a bug boffin?

Question 1)
WHAT IS PETTY POTTS'S NUMBER
PLATE?
A) POT5 72
B) SWITCH 1
C) POT6 73

Question 2)
PETTY POTTS TRIES TO ENTICE
SOME SQUIRRELS INTO TRYING HER
SWITCH FORMULA BUT HOW MANY
SQUIRRELS WERE IN THE PARK?
A) Four
B) Seven
C) One

Question 3)
HOW DO GRASSHOPPERS MAKE THEIR
CHIRRUP NOISE?
A) Singing
B) Rubbing their legs against their
bodies
C) Rubbing their wings together

Question 4)
WHAT PREDATOR DO JOSH AND
DANNY RUN INTO ON THEIR WAY TO
THE PARK?
A) Mouse
B) Cat
C) Fox

Question 5)
WHICH TYPE OF BIRD DO JOSH AND
DANNY HIDE FROM?
A) Starling
B) Blackbird
C) Kingfisher

Question 6)
BY THE END OF THE STORY, HOW
MANY REPTOSWITCH CUBES HAS
PETTY COLLECTED?
A) One
B) Three
C) Six

Question 7)
WHEN JOSH AND DANNY ARE
GRASSHOPPERS, WHAT DO THEY
DO TO TRY AND GET PETTY'S
ATTENTION?
A) Jump up and down on her head
B) Hold up a sign saying 'We are
down here!'
C) Disco dance

Question 8)
WHAT DOES MR GRANT SMELL OF?
A) Sour milk and cheese
B) Freshly cut grass and roses
C) Old tobacco and unwashed
socks

Answers on page 119

Answers

Word search (page 110)

S	W	I	T	C	H	E	F	O	U
C	T	D	X	N	S	Q	O	P	V
H	A	A	C	L	O	G	R	H	D
O	C	N	R	S	J	A	M	P	O
O	G	N	P	L	F	D	U	T	I
L	K	Y	L	B	I	L	L	Y	K
D	A	B	A	N	G	N	A	U	I
C	L	A	R	E	V	L	G	E	Y
Q	J	H	O	L	O	G	R	A	M
M	R	G	R	A	N	T	L	U	R

Spot the difference (page 111)

True or False (page 112)

1) True
2) True
3) True
4) False
5) True
6) False
7) False
8) False
9) True
10) False

Missing pieces (page 113)

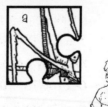

a

118

Answers

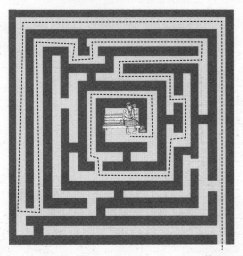

Maze (page 115)

Are you a bug boffin?
(page 117)
Answer 1) A
Answer 2) A
Answer 3) B
Answer 4) B
Answer 5) A
Answer 6) B
Answer 7) C
Answer 8) C

Give yourself a point for every
question you got right.
6–8 POINTS — You are a real bug
boffin! Nothing gets past you.
3–5 POINTS — You are SWITCHed on!
You enjoy a good adventure.
0–2 POINTS — Oh dear, looks as if you
need to brush up on your bug skills!
Better luck next time!

About the author

Ali Sparkes grew up in the woods of Hampshire. Actually, strictly speaking she grew up in a house in Hampshire. The woods were great but lacked basic facilities like sofas and a well stocked fridge. Nevertheless, the woods were where she and her friends spent much of their time and so Ali grew up with a deep and abiding love of wildlife. If you ever see Ali with a large garden spider on her shoulder she will most likely be screeching 'AAAAAAAAAARRRRRGHGETITOFFME!'

Ali lives in Southampton with her husband and sons and would never kill a creepy-crawly of any kind. They are more scared of her than she is of them. (Creepy-crawlies, not her husband and sons.)

Other books
in the  series

S.W.I.T.C.H.
SERUM WHICH INSTIGATES TOTAL CELLULAR HIJACK

Ali Sparkes — Illustrated by Ross Collins

S.W.I.T.C.H.
SERUM WHICH INSTIGATES TOTAL CELLULAR HIJACK

Spider Stampede

Ali Sparkes — Illustrated by Ross Collins

S.W.I.T.C.H.
SERUM WHICH INSTIGATES TOTAL CELLULAR HIJACK

Fly Frenzy

Ali Sparkes — Illustrated by Ross Collins

S.W.I.T.C.H.
SERUM WHICH INSTIGATES TOTAL CELLULAR HIJACK

Ant Attack

Ali Sparkes — Illustrated by Ross Collins

S.W.I.T.C.H.
SERUM WHICH INSTIGATES TOTAL CELLULAR HIJACK

Crane Fly Crash

Ali Sparkes — Illustrated by Ross Collins

S.W.I.T.C.H.
SERUM WHICH INSTIGATES TOTAL CELLULAR HIJACK

Beetle Blast

S.W.I.T.C.H.

SERUM WHICH INSTIGATES TOTAL CELLULAR HIJACK

Whether you're interested in insects
or terrified of tarantulas, you'll love the
S.W.I.T.C.H. website!

Find out more about the bugs in Josh
and Danny's adventures, enter fantastic
competitions, read the first chapters
of all of the S.W.I.T.C.H. books, and enjoy
creepy-crawly games and activities.

www.switch-books.co.uk